WANTED
DEAD or ALIVE

CAPTAIN CUT-THROAT
for countless crimes of
downright dastardliness
and despicable dishonesty
REWARD 100,000 Doubloons

WANTED
DEAD or ALIVE

SNEAKY M'SQUEAKY
For diabolical dirtiness
and disgusting delinquency
REWARD 40,000 Doubloons

WANTED
DEAD or ALIVE

STINKY O'BLEARY
for black-hearted badness
and beastly barbarity
REWARD 50,000 Doubloons

For Seth – J.E.

For Valentín and Matías, my favourite pirates! – P.B.

First published 2013 by Macmillan Children's Books
a division of Macmillan Publishers Limited
20 New Wharf Road, London N1 9RR
Basingstoke and Oxford
Associated companies throughout the world
www.panmacmillan.com

ISBN: 978-0-230-76050-9

Text copyright © Jonathan Emmett 2013
Illustrations copyright © Poly Bernatene 2013

Moral rights asserted.
You can find out more about Jonathan Emmett's books at
www.scribblestreet.co.uk

1 3 5 7 9 8 6 4 2

A CIP catalogue record for this book is available from the British Library.

Printed in China

WANTED
DEAD or ALIVE

DEAD-EYED DIRK
For scoundrelly subterfuge
and stinking skulduggery
REWARD 30,000 Doubloons

WANTED
BAKED or GRILLED

FINDUS SPEW
for culinary cunning
and criminal cookery
REWARD 20,000 Doubloons

WANTED
DEAD or ALIVE

BLUE-BOTTOMED BART
For mean misconduct and
monstrous mischief
REWARD 50,000 Doubloons

WANTED
DEAD or ALIVE

QUILLY VON SQUINT
for reprehensible rudeness
and repulsive roguery
REWARD 50,000 Doubloons

WANTED
DEAD or ALIVE

DAISY CORTEZ
for frightful foulness
and fiendish felony
REWARD 60,000 Doubloons

Jonathan
Emmett

Poly
Bernatene

HERE BE MONSTERS

WANTED
DEAD or ALIVE

PREFERABLY
DEAD

CAPTAIN CUT-THROAT
for countless crimes of
downright dastardliness
and despicable dishonesty
REWARD 100,000 Doubloons

MACMILLAN CHILDREN'S BOOKS

Captain Cut-Throat was a pirate and a fearless pirate too.
He had the fastest pirate ship and the fiercest pirate crew.
He was the meanest mariner to sail the Seven Seas,
And everyone that met him went all wobbly at the knees.

Now Cut-Throat, he loved treasure, as every pirate should,
And he'd do anything to get some, sail anywhere he could.

So when he heard tell of an island, concealed in murky mist,
That was strewn with GIANT GEMSTONES — well how could he resist?

"With such treasure," growled the Captain, "we'd be rich forevermore."
"We must set sail for this island!" But his crew were not so sure.

"But here be monsters!" said the first mate. "Monsters hiding in the mist!"
"Nonsense!" growled the Captain. "Monsters simply don't exist."

So despite the mate's misgivings, they set sail that very day,
And with a fair wind in their favour, they were quickly on their way.

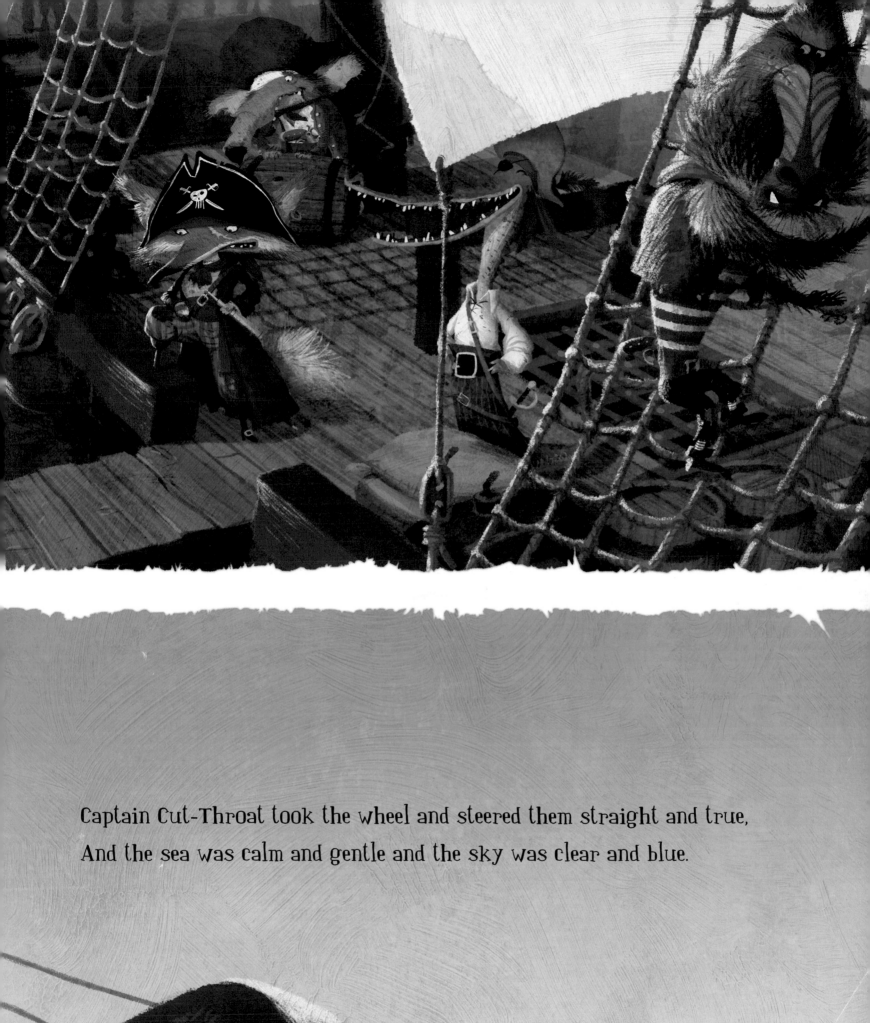

Captain Cut-Throat took the wheel and steered them straight and true,
And the sea was calm and gentle and the sky was clear and blue.

So the first half of the voyage passed without a hitch,
As the crew talked of the gemstones and how they'd all be rich.

And any thoughts of monsters were easily dismissed,
And everything was shipshape until they reached . . .

. . . THE MIST!

It lay across the ocean like a fearful foggy screen,

A wall of wispy whiteness through which nothing could be seen.

But they could hear the strangest noises, coming from within,

Wailing, hissing, squawking sounds — a most disturbing din!

"Turn back!"

cried the lookout as he gazed into the gloom.

"Turn back!"

cried the ship's cook. "Or we'll surely meet our doom!"

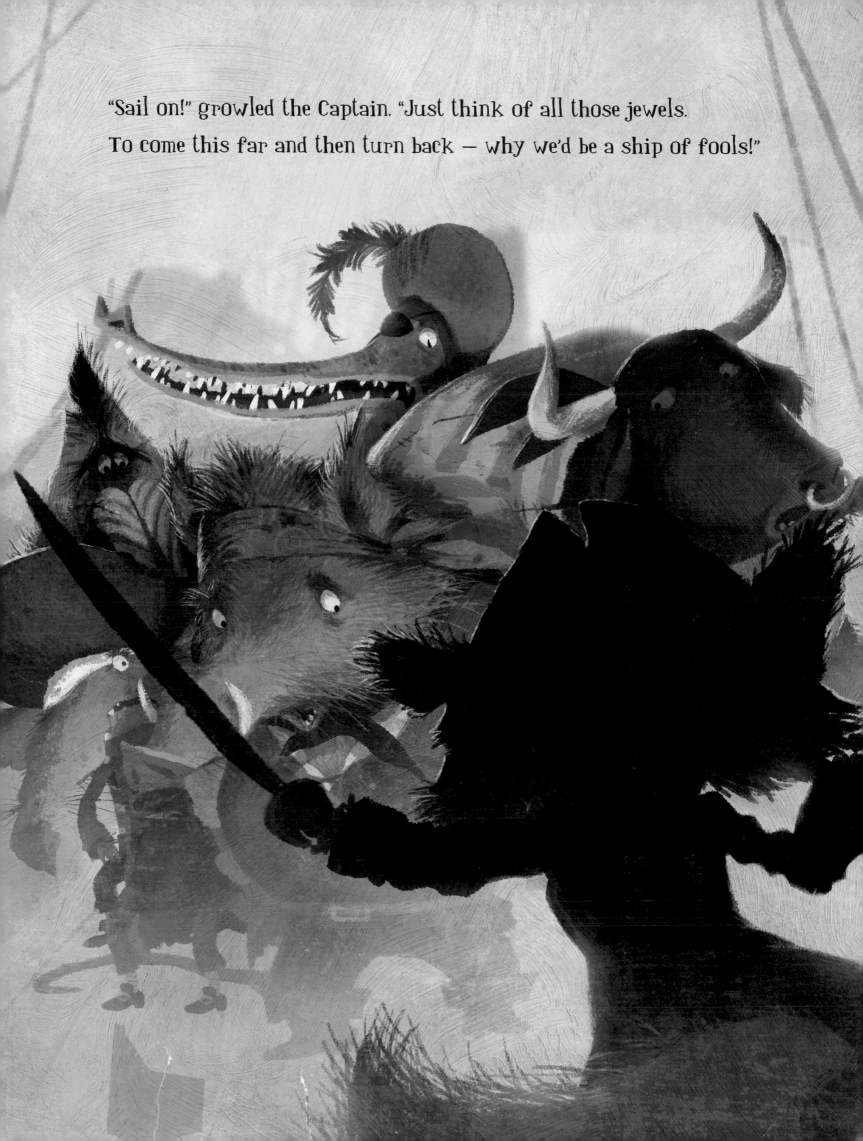

"Sail on!" growled the Captain. "Just think of all those jewels.
To come this far and then turn back — why we'd be a ship of fools!"

So on they sailed into the mist, the swirling whirling white,
Which swept in from above them and hid the sails from sight.
Then something swooped down through the air and perched upon the mast.
Something with a savage beak, something fierce and fast.

"Here be
monsters!"

cried the lookout.
"UP HERE! Inside the mist!"

"Nonsense!" growled the Captain.
"Monsters simply don't exist."

And the Captain didn't notice as hidden from his view,
Something FAT and FEATHERY snatched a clawful of the crew . . .

So on they sailed into the mist, the swirling whirling white,
Which swept in through the portholes and hid the hold from sight.
Then something burrowed through the hull and broke in from beneath,
Something smooth and slippery, with far too many teeth.

"Here be monsters!"

cried the ship's cook.
"DOWN HERE! Inside the mist!"

"Nonsense!" growled the Captain.
"Monsters simply don't exist."

And the Captain was oblivious, he didn't have a clue,

As something STRONG and SNAKELIKE took a mouthful of the crew . . .

So on they sailed into the mist, the swirling whirling white,
Which swept in all around them and hid the deck from sight.
Then something bumped against the bow and slithered up the side,
Something huge and hungry, something evil-eyed.

"Here be
monsters!"
cried the first mate.

"OVER HERE! Inside the mist!"

"Nonsense!" growled the Captain.
"Monsters simply don't exist."

And the Captain, he did nothing, for what was there to do?
As something TALL and TENTACLED polished off the crew.

On the Captain sailed alone and the mist began to clear,
And the outline of an island started slowly to appear.
"LAND HO!" growled the Captain, but the crew did not reply,
And Cut-Throat was ashore before he stopped to wonder why.

"They must have all abandoned ship, the yellow-bellied scum.
Those blubbering little babies — they've scarpered home to mum!"

"How silly," growled the Captain, "to come this far and flee.
Well, if they don't want treasure, then that's all the more for me!"

For the isle was jammed with giant gems, crammed from shore to shore.
There must have been a hundred — no a thousand — maybe more!
"Mine, all mine!" The Captain cried as he jumped with joy and greed.
"More gems than I could ever want, more gems than I could need!"

But as the Captain stomped his feet
and danced upon the ground,
The gemstones stirred around him
and made a cracking sound . . .

And out popped teeth and tentacles, and out popped claws and legs,
For what he'd thought were giant jewels, were really . . .

. . . GIANT
EGGS!

"HERE BE MONSTERS!" cried the Captain. "ALL AROUND ME, IN THE MIST!"

"HERE BE MONSTERS!" wailed the Captain. "MONSTERS REALLY **DO** EXIST!"

But there was no one there to hear him, not a soul for miles around,
Or no one that was able to understand the sound.

Captain Cut-Throat was a pirate and a fearless pirate too.

He had the fastest pirate ship and the fiercest pirate crew.

He was the meanest mariner, the baddest of the bunch.

Captain Cut-Throat WAS a pirate — but he ended up as . . .

. . . LUNCH!